BIG
BAD
WOLF
IS GOOD

Published in 2002 by Sterling Publishing Co., Inc.
387 Park Avenue South
New York, NY 10016

First published in 2001 in Great Britain by
Gullane Children's Books

Distributed in Canada by Sterling Publishing
c/o Canadian Manda Group, One Atlantc Avenue, Suite 105
Toronto, Ontario, Canada M6K 3E7

Text © Simon Puttock 2001
Illustrations © Lynne Chapman 2001

Simon Puttock and Lynne Chapman have the moral right
to be identified as the author and illustrator of this work.

For Shaun, Isabel
and Alexander Joseph
Fernando Addison Marcos,
with love
S.P.

For René and Derek
L.C.

BIG
BAD
WOLF
IS GOOD

Simon Puttock

Illustrated by

Lynne Chapman

Sterling Publishing Co., Inc.
New York

Big Bad Wolf was lonely. He had no friends.
"Perhaps it's because I'm big and scary," he said
to himself. "Perhaps it's because I'm bad, bad, bad."
He sat and he thought and he thought.

"I know," he said, "I will not be bad anymore.
I will be good. Then someone will be my friend."
So Big Bad Wolf set off to be good.

Mrs Goose was in the garden with her seven little goslings. "Good day," said Big Bad Wolf, politely raising his hat.

"HONK!" cried Mrs Goose, "It's Big Bad Wolf!"
Mrs Goose and her seven little goslings ran
into the house and slammed the door.

"Oh, Mrs Goose," said Big Bad Wolf sweetly,
"please open the door. I'm a good wolf now, and
I've come to play with your seven little goslings."
But Mrs Goose would not open the door.

The seven little goslings chanted. . .
"Big Bad Wolf, stay away and
DON'T come back another day!"
And they made faces through the curtains.

Big Bad Wolf felt sad. Those geese had not given him a chance. He sat and he thought and he thought. "I know," he said, "I will be useful and good. Then someone will be my friend."

So Big Bad Wolf set out
to be useful and good.

Mrs Chicken was going out. She was waiting for the babysitter for her six little chicks. "Where can that babysitter be?" she fussed.

"Ahem!" Big Bad Wolf coughed politely. "I would be glad to sit with your six little chicks."

"YIKES!" squawked Mrs Chicken,
"It's Big Bad Wolf! Run, children, run!"
They ran into the house and slammed the door.

"Oh, Mrs Chicken," said Big Bad Wolf sweetly,
"I'm a good wolf now. Please let me in to
look after your six little chicks."
But Mrs Chicken would not open the door.

The six little chicks chanted. . .
"Big Bad Wolf, stay away and don't
come back – EVER AGAIN!"
And they made faces through the curtains.

Big Bad Wolf was really sad. Those chickens had not given him a chance. He sat and he thought and he thought and he thought.

"I know," he said, "I will be useful and good, and I will do a noble deed. Then someone will surely be my friend."

So Big Bad Wolf set off to be useful
and good, and to do a noble deed.

Mrs Duck stood on her doorstep calling, "Where are you, Number Five?"

"Good evening, Mrs Duck," said Big Bad Wolf, bowing politely, "What seems to be the trouble? May I be of some assistance?"

Mrs Duck flew into a rage. "QUACK!"
she cried, "It's Big Bad Wolf and he's
eaten poor little Number Five!"
   She rushed inside and
slammed the door.

Big Bad Wolf was upset. He banged
and banged at Mrs Duck's door.
   "Let me in," he howled,
"I haven't eaten anybody!"
But Mrs Duck would not open the door.

The little ducklings One to Four sang. . .
"Big Bad Wolf, stay away, and DON'T come
back because you've EATEN Number Five!"
And they made sad faces at him through the curtains.

"Eaten Number Five indeed!" shouted Big Bad Wolf. "I'll show them! I won't be good, I'll be BAD, BAD, BAD!" Big Bad Wolf was stamping through the woods in a terrible temper when he heard a small, sad voice.

"Quack, I'm lost," said the voice.
Big Bad Wolf stepped out from behind a tree.
"Quack!" cried Number Five, "Quack, Quack, HELP!
It's Big Bad Wolf and he's going to EAT ME!"

Big Bad Wolf's feelings were horribly hurt.
"If you don't stop being silly *this* minute," he roared,
"I *will* eat you. So there!"

Number Five looked up.
A fat little tear rolled down his bill.
"I want my mommy," he said.
"There, there," said Big Bad Wolf,
"we'll find your mommy."

And he scooped up
Number Five and put
him in his pocket.

Big Bad Wolf knocked at Mrs Duck's door.
  "Excuse me," he called sweetly, "I've found Number Five."
The door opened a tiny crack.
  "Have you really?" asked Mrs Duck.
  "Really and truly," said Big Bad Wolf.
  "And you haven't eaten him?" asked Mrs Duck.

When Mrs Duck saw her lost
little duckling, she snatched him
inside and shut the front door, BANG!

Big Bad Wolf walked away sadly.
He had been useful *and*
good *and* he'd done a noble deed, but
STILL nobody wanted to be his friend.
A big, fat tear rolled down his nose.

"Oh, Big Bad Wolf," cried Mrs Duck,
opening the front door wide.
Big Bad Wolf stopped.
"Would you like to come inside
for a cup of tea?" she asked.
Big Bad Wolf turned round.
"Yes, please," he sniffed.

Big Bad Wolf had a lovely visit. He drank
three cups of tea and ate eleven cookies.
Then he played with the ducklings, One to Five.

"Thank you, Mrs Duck," said
Big Bad Wolf, when it was time to go home.
"Oh, thank *you*, Big Bad Wolf," said Mrs Duck,
"for finding Duckling Number Five. You are a hero!"
"Do you think," asked Big Bad Wolf shyly, "that
you could call me Big *Good* Wolf now?"

Mrs Duck laughed. "Don't be silly,"
she said and she gave him a big, warm hug.
"You will always be Big Bad Wolf.
But you are *good*, too!"

J
E
PUTTOCK

11/08